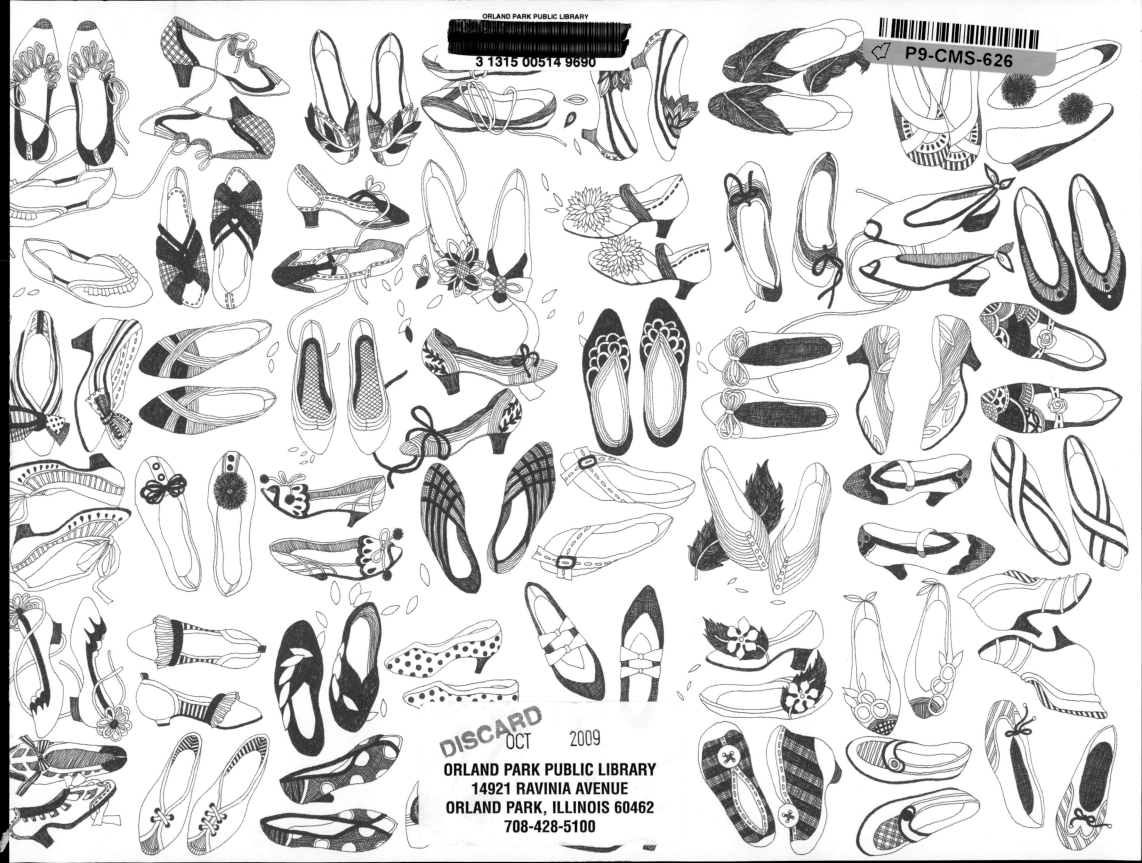

For those who are brave enough to wear red shoes.
S.Y.

For Lola and Miles and all their creative endeavors,
and for both of my shoe loving Angelas.
G.F.

The Red Shoes

Illustrated by Sun Young Yoo & Written by Gloria Fowler

AMMO
AMERICAN MODERN **BOOKS**

There once was a girl named Karen whose mother was the town shoemaker. And although they did not have much money, they both had creativity to spare. Every day Karen would play in her mother's tiny old shop and dream about making beautiful dancing shoes and clothes to go with them.

Although her mother could not afford to buy Karen hardly anything at all, she had been secretly making a pair of lovely red shoes for Karen's birthday from some leftover scraps of red leather.

When the pair of shoes was almost done, Karen's mother fell gravely ill and soon after passed away. A brokenhearted Karen wore the red shoes for the first time to her mother's funeral. From then on whenever Karen tried to escape her sorrow, she would wear the red shoes and dance into the forest, remembering her mother's joyful spirit and wishing that she was still alive.

It was on one of these days, that a queen and her daughter from a faraway land came passing through the village. The young princess caught site of Karen's red shoes and coveted them so. The queen ordered her servants to take them from Karen, but the shoes had grown fast to her feet. In contrast to Karen, the princess was spoiled and ill-mannered and demanded the red shoes.

The queen proclaimed that if in three days Karen did not turn over the red shoes, the executioner would have to cut off her feet to remove them. Karen wanted to remove the shoes and give them to the queen, but at the same time feared that all of her memories of her mother, and all of her own dreams and desires, would disappear if the red shoes left her.

Karen was distraught. She sat at the edge of the river by the forest and cried and cried. Finally, as she washed her tears away, she looked at her own reflection in the water and saw her mother's kind and loving image looking back at her. Karen knew at once what she must do.

She ran back to the village and to her mother's tiny old shop. At once she began to search in all the dusty shelves for scraps of leather, buttons, beads, sequins, and thread. She worked feverishly for three days and nights. It was as if her mother's hands were guiding her own.

As she sewed the last stitch, the red shoes she was still wearing fell off of her feet. She now realized that she could let go, and even if she lost the red shoes, she would never lose the infinite amount of love and confidence her mother had in her. She put on the pair of new shoes, picked up the red shoes, and bravely walked outside just in time to see the queen and her daughter arrive.

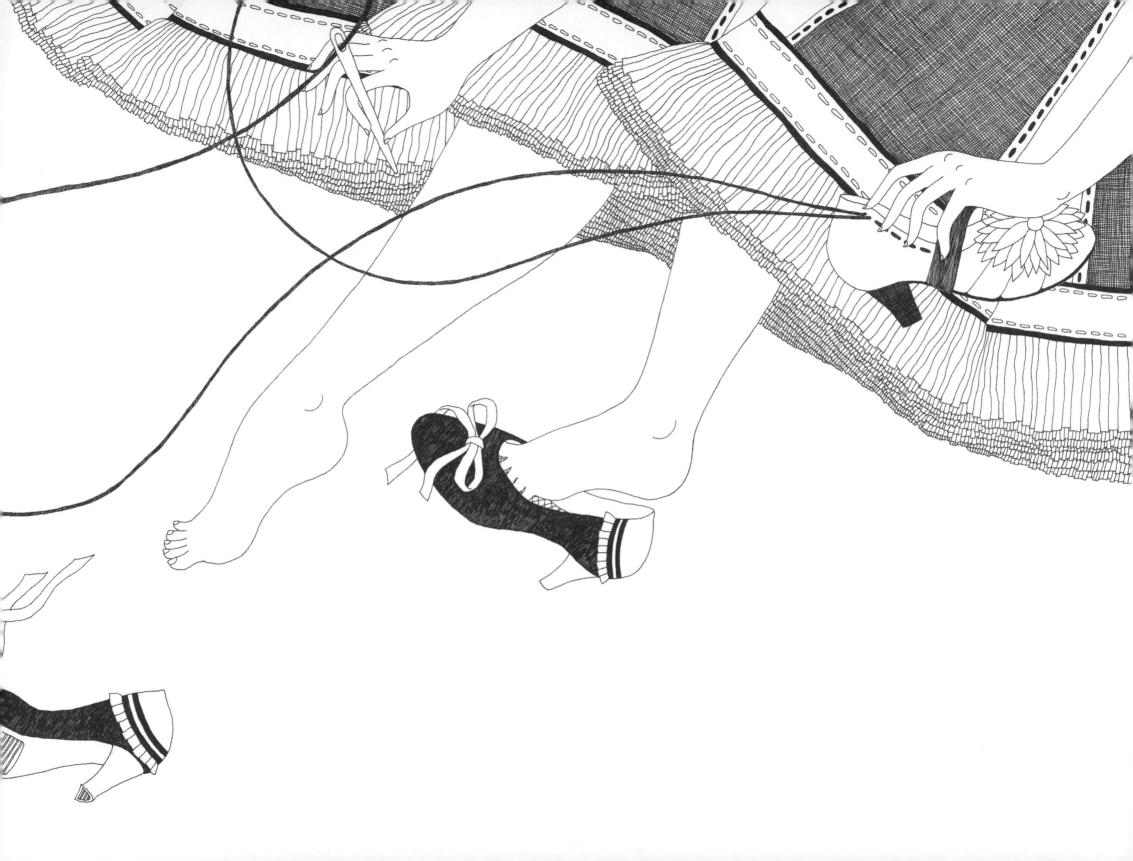

As the townspeople gathered around, Karen graciously began to hand over the pair of red shoes. Alas, the fickle and spoiled young princess now saw the beautiful pair of new shoes that Karen was wearing and declared that she wanted those instead.

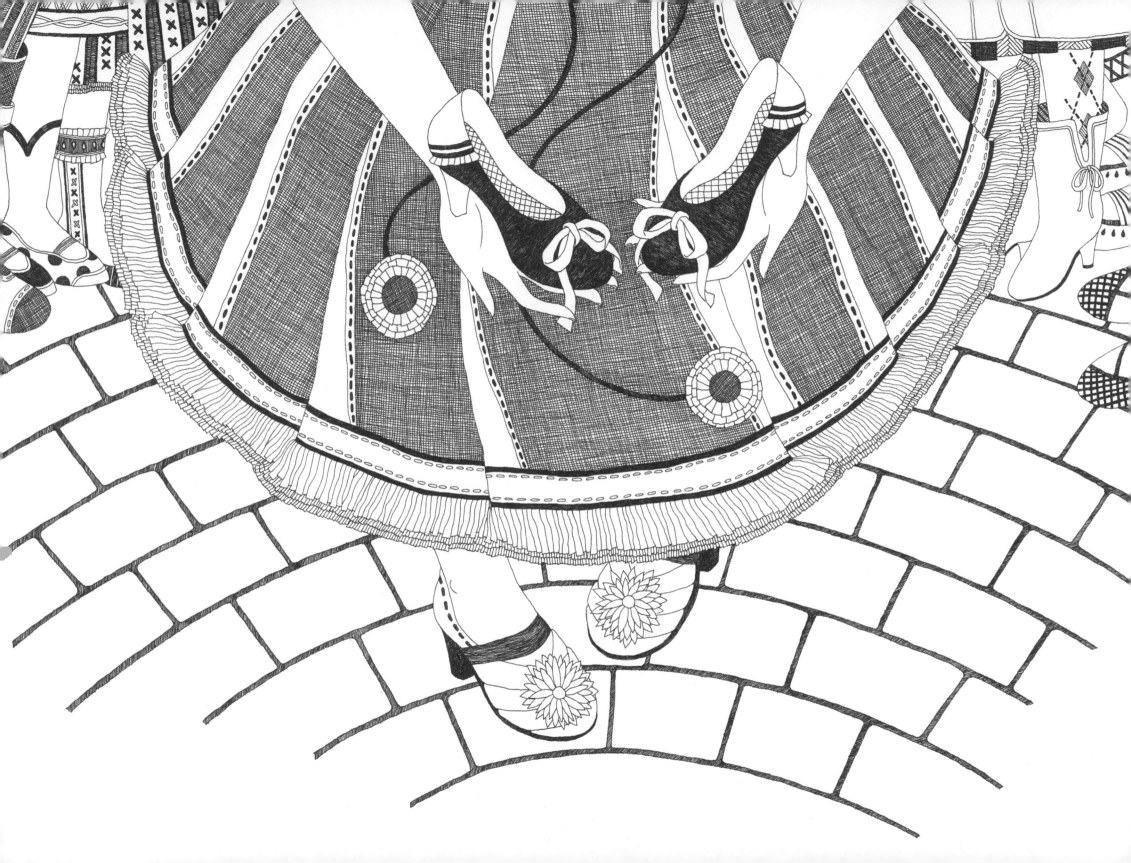

Finding her strength, Karen calmly said, very well, but that they would cost a satchel full of gold coins. At first the queen was furious, but as her annoying daughter continued to beg her mother for them, the queen finally relented and properly paid Karen for the shoes. All of the townspeople, as well as the queen's servants, were pleased for Karen.

As for Karen, not only was she able to keep her beloved red shoes, but she also earned a well-deserved amount of money for which she already had a special plan in mind, one that would satisfy her own heart's desire.

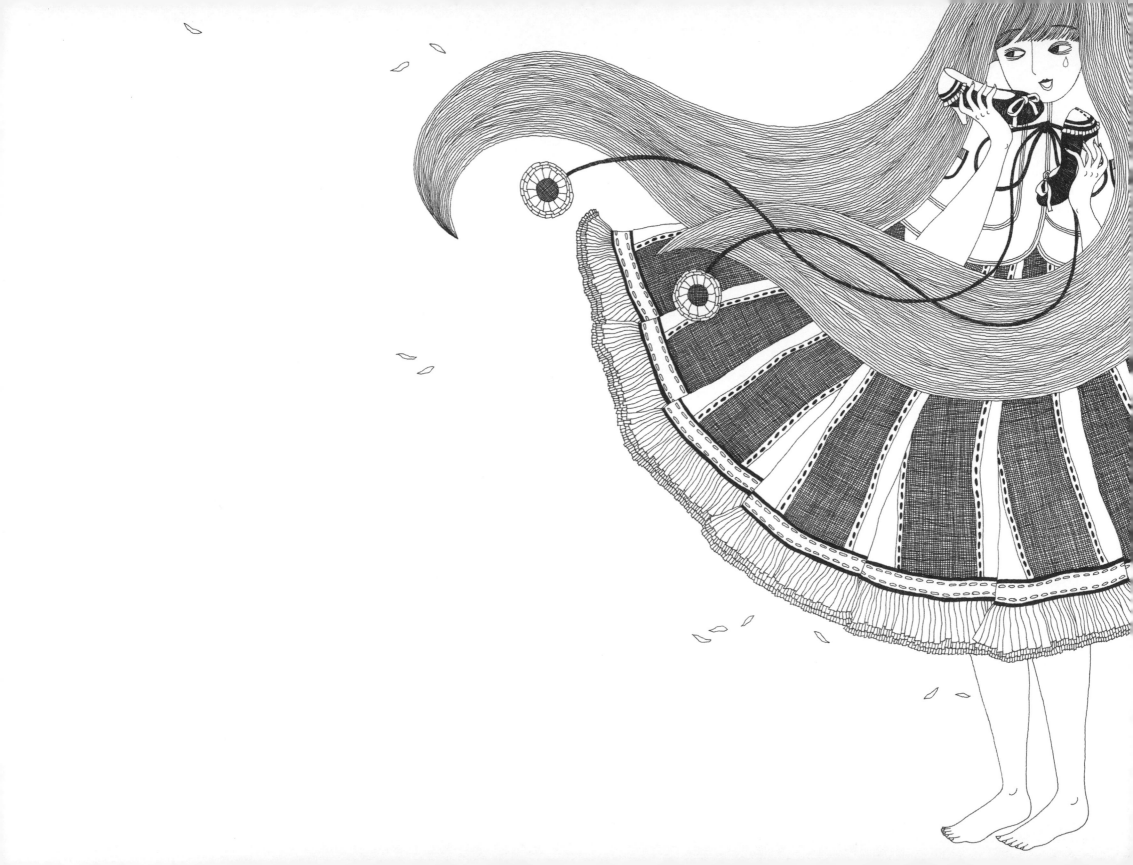

A year passed and then another, and one day the same queen and her daughter passed through the village in their carriage. They stopped abruptly at a storefront with an ornate sign over it that read "The Red Shoes."

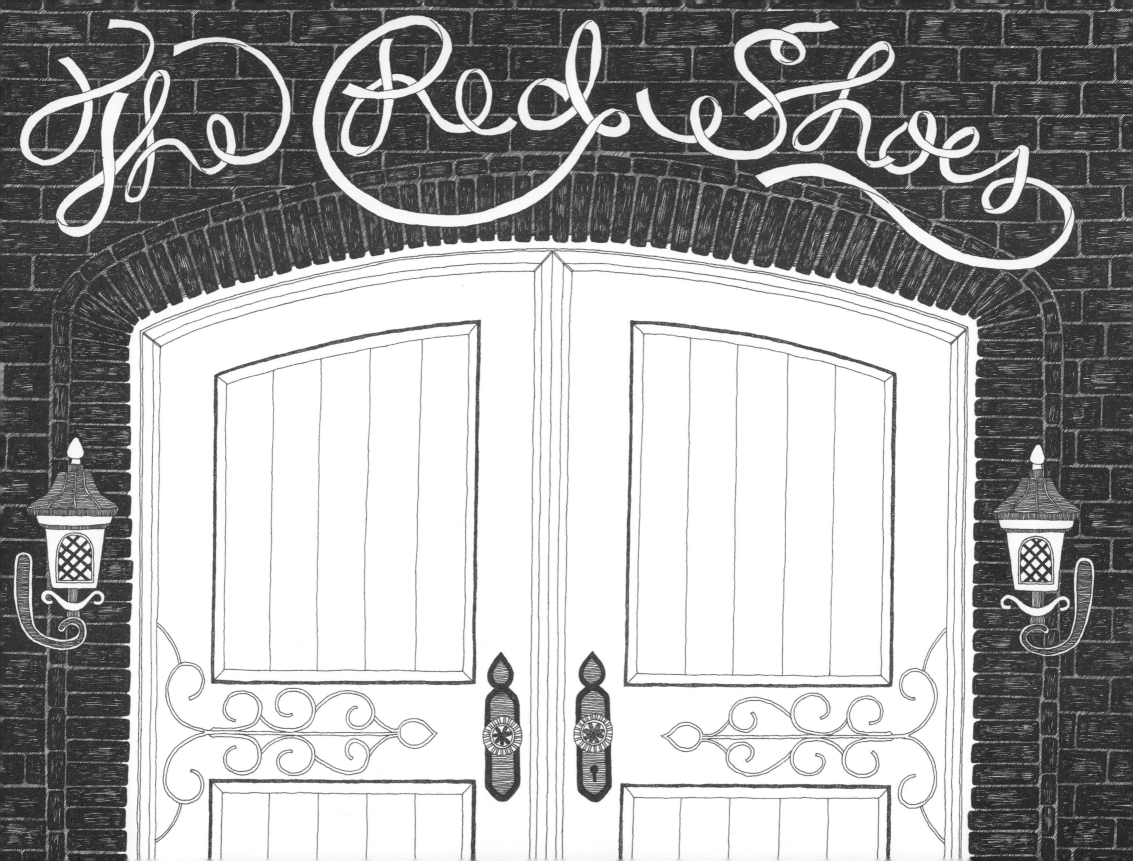

As the heavy wooden double doors opened, they walked in and soon discovered what many others already had: Karen's very own shop with dozens and dozens of the most beautiful and original handmade shoes in all the land. There were shoes made of velvet and shoes made of satin; there were shoes with laces and shoes with ribbons, shoes with sequins, and even a pair with real red rubies. All of them came from Karen's own imagination, creativity, and hard work.

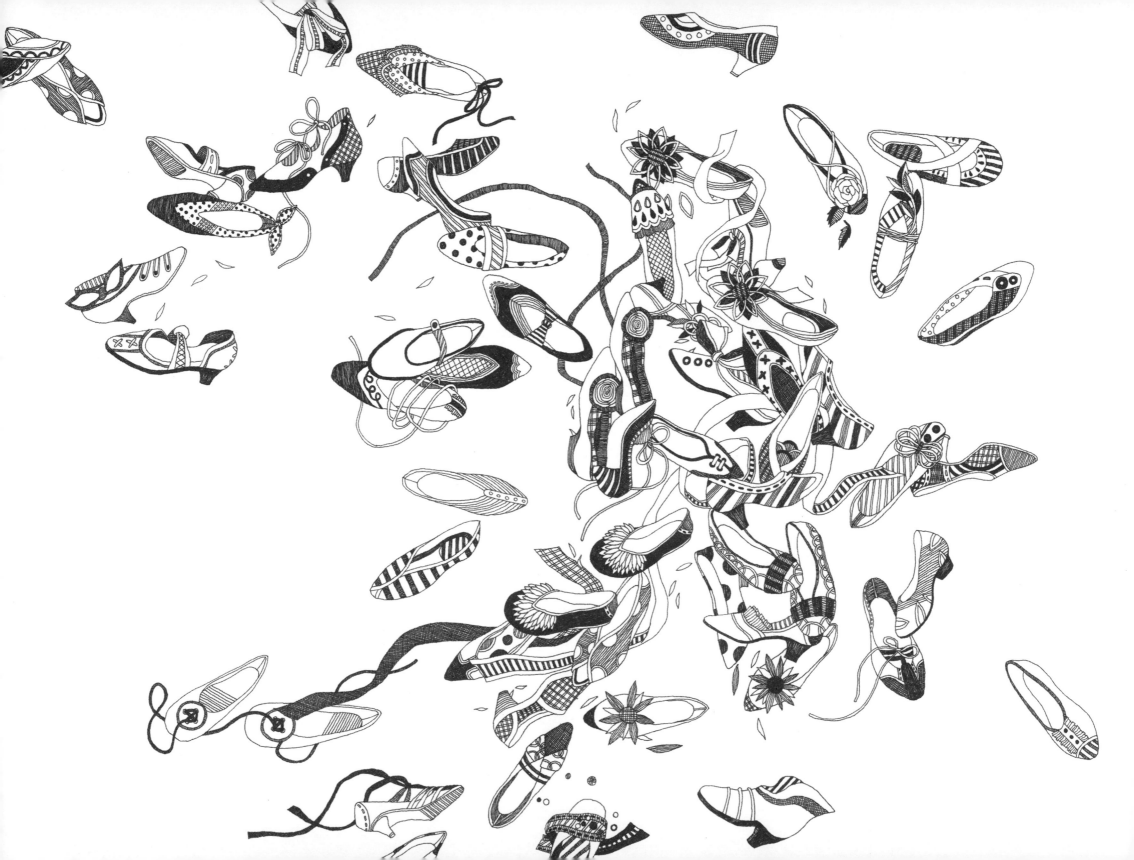

All of this pleased Karen so, and she shyly smiled to herself and wondered what she would dream up next.

THE RED SHOES

E
FOW

Illustrated by Sun Young Yoo
Written by Gloria Fowler
Based on the original story *The Red Shoes* by Hans Christian Andersen

Art Direction by Gloria Fowler and Steve Crist
Book Design by Sun Young Yoo
Typeset in Mrs Eaves Roman and Petite Caps
Production by Reid Embrey

Distributed in the USA and CANADA by Ingram Publisher Services
www.ingrampublisherservices.com

Distributed in the UK by ORCA Book Services
www.orcabookservices.co.uk

ISBN 9781934429068
Library of Congress Control Number 2008931756

Printed in China

To purchase additional copies of *The Red Shoes*, or for more information on AMMO Books, please visit our website at www.ammobooks.com

AMERICAN MODERN **BOOKS**

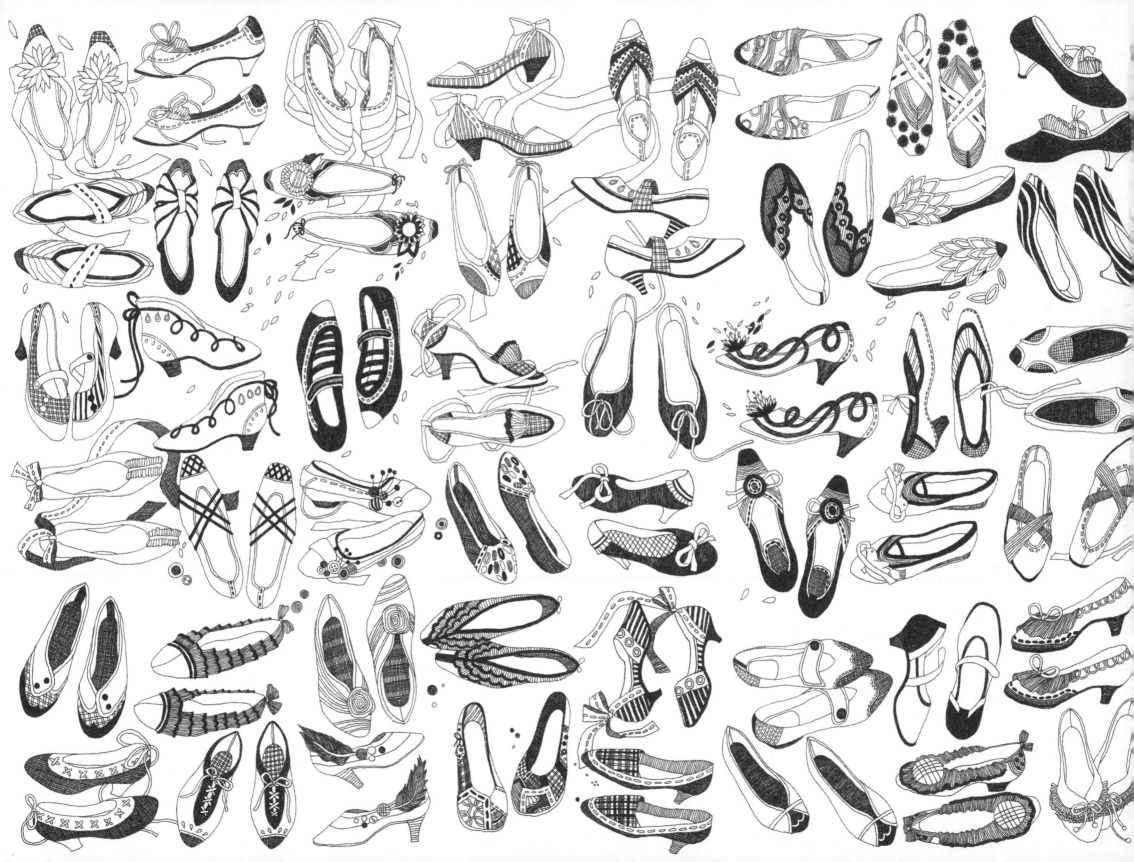